BJ GOES ON
HOLIDAY

By Stan Cullimore

Illustrated by Karen Hayles

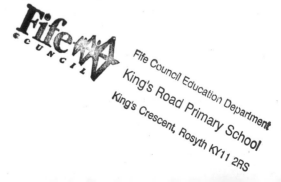

Chapter 1

We're All Going - On A Summer Holiday!

One cold, wet, Saturday morning in February the four members of the Buckett household were sitting round the breakfast table eating breakfast - at least, some of them were eating breakfast.

Some of them were more interested in trying to decide what to do with themselves for the rest of the day.

"We could always go out for a walk," suggested BJ.

Mrs Buckett sighed. "I'm afraid it's too wet for that, BJ. Sorry." She looked over at her husband. "Has anybody else got any ideas as to what we could do today?"

There was no reply.

Mr Buckett was too busy eating. He was also too busy trying to hide behind his newspaper.

His wife sighed. "I didn't think you would have any ideas, Henry." She shook her head. "The only thing you seem to be interested in today is that silly newspaper of yours."

She took a piece of toast from the rack in front of her and spread marmalade over it.

Still her husband said nothing.

"I don't know what you're reading about," said Mrs Buckett. "But it must be very interesting." She shook her head and took a bite of toast.

In fact, for once, Mrs Buckett was wrong. Her husband was not in the least bit interested in his newspaper. Not at all.

He was far more interested in the Rice Krispies.

"Psst," hissed Mr Buckett. "Johnny. Can you pass me the Rice Krispies again?"

But Johnny didn't hear him – which wasn't really surprising, because Mr Buckett was whispering.

And in case you are wondering why he was whispering I'll tell you.

He was whispering because he had already eaten two big bowls full of his favourite cereal, and he didn't want his wife to realise that he was about to have a third!

For, if she found out, she would tell him off for being greedy, and then give him a lecture about Getting Fat In His Old Age.

"Johnny," repeated his father, slightly louder this time. "Can you please pass me the Rice Krispies?" He gritted his teeth. "Please!"

"Huh?" Johnny turned to look at his father. "What did you say, Dad?"

Dad rolled his eyes, and waved his arm from side to side in a desperate attempt to tell his son to keep his voice down. If his wife overheard them talking and realised what he was up to he was in big trouble.

BJ, who was still looking out of the window at the rain pouring down outside, coughed.

"Dad asked if you could pass him the Rice Krispies," he said, clearly. "I think he wants to have some more," he added helpfully.

Dad put his fingers to his lips. "Ssh," he hissed. "Keep your voice down."

But it was too late.

His wife had already heard what was going on. She put down the piece of toast she was holding and frowned at the top of her husband's head, which was the only part of him that she could see over the newspaper.

"How many bowls of Rice Krispies have you had, Henry?" she asked.

Mr Buckett groaned. Then he slowly folded up his newspaper and tried to look innocent. It didn't work.

"Pardon, dear?" he said. "What did you say? I didn't hear you. I was too busy reading my newspaper."

His wife tutted. "I don't believe a word of it. You are supposed to be thinking of things for us to do today. Aren't you?"

Mr Buckett looked genuinely surprised. "Am I?"

"Yes, you are. And instead, what do I find? I find that you've been stuffing your face with cereals." Mrs Buckett snorted. "You mark my words, Henry Buckett. If you're not careful you'll end up Getting Fat In Your Old Age."

Mr Buckett tried to look innocent again. And failed, again. "What do you mean - stuffing my face with cereals? I haven't been stuffing my face with cereals, have I Johnny?"

Just then, Johnny, who was busy reading a comic and not listening to the conversation between his parents, picked up the Rice Krispies packet and handed it to his father.

"Here you are, Dad." He looked up. "Hey, how many bowls of cereal have you had?"

"Two," replied BJ. "This one will be his third."

Henry Buckett opened his mouth to speak, and then decided not to bother. Instead, he took the packet from his son and smiled weakly at his wife.

There were a few seconds of silence.

"I wasn't really going to have any more, you know," he said, eventually. "That would have been greedy."

His wife raised an eyebrow. "What were you going to do then?" she asked.

Suddenly Mr Buckett had a brainwave. He stood up. "I was going to clear the table," he said quickly. Then, still holding the Rice Krispies packet, he ran out of the room.

"That stupid dog," he muttered, when he got into the safety of the kitchen. "Every time it opens its mouth, it gets me into trouble! What I need is a rest, before that dog sends me mad."

Just then, there was a clunk from the porch.

"That must be the post arriving," said BJ happily. He wagged his tail. "Can I go and get it?"

Mrs Bucket smiled, and nodded at the little dog. "Of course you can, BJ. You always fetch the letters."

BJ grinned. "I know!" Then he jumped down from his chair and ran along the hallway.

When he got back, he dropped a large white envelope onto the table in front of Mrs Buckett. "It's for you," he said.

Mr Buckett poked his head round the kitchen door. "Anything interesting?" he asked.

"No," replied his wife. "It's just a summer holiday brochure."

Mr Buckett looked thoughtful. "Oh, that's good."

"What's so good about it?" asked his wife. "I thought we had already agreed that we weren't going to have a summer holiday this year. You said that we couldn't afford it."

Mr Buckett looked even more thoughtful. "Well," he said slowly, "I think we can now."

"Really?" gasped Johnny.

His father nodded. "Yes, I don't see why not."

"But I don't understand," said Mrs Buckett, frowning. "You told me that we had lots of bills to pay at the moment, so we couldn't afford to spend any more money."

Her husband nodded. "You're right. I thought that we had lots of bills to pay, but I must have been wrong – we haven't been sent any bills for weeks, which means we've got some money saved in the bank."

Mrs Buckett smiled. "That is good." She liked having money in the bank – it meant that she could spend it.

Suddenly, Mr Buckett had a Brilliant Idea. "I know what we should do today," he said.

"What?" asked his wife.

"We should go to the travel agents and book ourselves a nice summer holiday somewhere foreign."

"Yippee," cried BJ. "I've never been on a summer holiday before."

Dad turned and walked back into the kitchen. "And you won't be going on this one either," he muttered under his breath. "Not if I can help it! The only way I'm going to get peace and quiet is if you don't come along with us."

He smiled. "Which is why I want to go on a foreign holiday. You aren't allowed to take dogs with you on foreign holidays..."

Three quarters of an hour later, after Dad had finished the washing up and Johnny had tidied his room, all four members of the household met in the hallway.

"Right," said Dad rubbing his hands together, "are we all ready to go to the travel agents, then? I've got the car out."

He opened the cupboard under the stairs and reached in to get his coat. "Come on," he said cheerfully. "Follow me."

"Hold on a minute, Henry," said his wife. "Not so fast. There are a couple of things we have to sort out before we leave the house."

Inside the cupboard under the stairs, Mr Buckett silently pulled a face. He didn't like it when his wife said that there were 'a couple of things to sort out'. It usually meant that she had totally changed her mind about something they had already agreed on.

"What things do we have to sort out?" he asked nervously.

"Nothing much," replied his wife.

Mr Buckett sighed. "Thank goodness for that."

"I was just wondering. Perhaps we shouldn't have an expensive summer holiday after all. I mean, Auntie Mary did offer to lend us her tent so we could go camping in Devon, didn't she?"

Her husband groaned. "But I hate camping!"

"Did you say camping?" asked Johnny.

His mother nodded.

"Brilliant," he cried. "I love camping." He bent down and rubbed BJ behind the ears. "And so will you!"

BJ nodded happily. "Oh, I do," he shouted, full of beans. "I do."

With that, he jumped onto the telephone table and began to leap around, getting more and more excited and barking at the top of his voice.

Suddenly, he slipped and fell right off the edge of the table.

"Are you all right, BJ?" asked Johnny.

BJ chuckled. "Yep. I just got a bit excited, that's all."

Johnny bent down and picked him up with a look of mild surprise on his face. "I'm not surprised. I didn't know that you'd been camping before though, BJ."

BJ grinned at him through his monocle and shook his head. "I haven't been camping before."

"Then how do you know you like it?"

BJ shrugged happily. "I was guessing."

Johnny burst out laughing. "Honestly, BJ, you do the strangest things sometimes."

"I know I do. Watch this."

BJ squirmed out of Johnny's arms and leapt down onto the carpet. Then he began racing up and down the hallway shouting at the top of his voice. "We're going camping. We're going camping! Yippee, yippee."

Dad, who had been listening to all this in silence, coughed quietly.

BJ ignored him.

Dad coughed again, louder this time.

BJ still ignored him.

"I said," said Dad in a loud voice, "cough, cough."

BJ stopped racing around and put his head on one side. He looked at Mr Buckett thoughtfully, through his monocle. "You know what I think, Mr Buckett?" he said eventually. "I think you've got a cough coming on."

Mrs Buckett nodded. "He's right, Henry. You do sound like you've got a cough coming on. Have you been riding your bicycle again without wearing your helmet?"

Dad groaned. "No, I haven't been riding my bicycle without my helmet. And nor have I got a stupid cough coming on! I'm only trying to draw your attention to the one fact that you all seem to have forgotten."

Mrs Buckett frowned. "What's that, dear?"

"I hate camping. I don't want to go on a camping holiday to Devon."

"Why ever not?" asked Mrs Buckett. "Think how much money we would save."

"I don't want to save money. I want to spend it. I want to have a nice, peaceful summer holiday in a place that is hot, and has got a beach for me to lie on and where the sun always shines."

Johnny nodded. "Sounds good to me."

His mother smiled. "I agree – so we'll go to Devon, shall we?"

"No," shouted her husband. "I don't want to go to Devon. I want to go on a foreign holiday."

"But dear," said his wife gently. "If we went on a foreign holiday, BJ wouldn't be able to come with us. They don't allow you to take dogs on foreign holidays."

"Precisely," shouted Mr Buckett, throwing his hands into the air. "I don't want that wretched animal to come with us!"

For a few seconds, nobody spoke. Then, at last, BJ cleared his throat. "So, do I take it that you don't want me to come on holiday with you then, Mr Buckett?"

He sniffed, sadly.

Mr Buckett lowered his hands and looked round at the faces of his family. They did not look very impressed.

"Well, er..., what I mean to say is, er..." He stopped and licked his lips. He could tell that it wasn't going to be easy to get out of this one.

"What I mean to say," he repeated "is, er..." He stopped again.

"Yes, Henry. Tell us – what do you mean to say?" asked his wife sweetly.

Mr Buckett coughed. "Er..." He thought quickly, but nothing came to him. Suddenly he remembered an old saying of his father's. 'When all else fails – try using the truth.' He took a deep breath.

"What I mean to say is this. I want a nice, peaceful, relaxing holiday – we can afford it, after all – can't we?"

His wife nodded. "Yes, we all want a nice, peaceful, relaxing holiday – all of us, Henry. And that includes BJ."

Mr Buckett gulped. "I know," he said nervously. "But the trouble is, it seems to me, that every time BJ opens his mouth he gets me into trouble!"

Mrs Buckett raised an eyebrow. "Really?" she asked quietly.

Her husband nodded. "Yes, look at this morning, for example. The minute he opened his mouth and went on about Rice Krispies, you gave me a row for being greedy."

"But you were being greedy, weren't you?"

Mr Buckett opened his mouth to argue, and then noticed the look on his wife's face. He decided not to bother. She was not in a mood to be argued with.

Also, he had just realised that she was right.

"Yes, dear," he mumbled.

"So BJ didn't get you into trouble. Your greediness got you into trouble, didn't it?"

"Yes, dear."

"So, let's not hear any more about going on holiday and leaving BJ behind. Do I make myself clear?"

Mr Buckett nodded again. All of a sudden he felt guilty. Perhaps he had been a bit harsh on BJ after all.

"But what about all the money we've got saved up in the bank?" he asked, miserably.

His wife smiled. "Don't you worry about that, dear." She patted him on the hand. "I'm sure we'll be able to think of something to spend it on, won't we, BJ?"

She looked around.

BJ was nowhere to be seen.

"BJ?" she called. "Where are you, BJ?"

"He's gone up to my room," muttered Johnny, who was sitting on the bottom stair. "I think he's really hurt by what Dad said." He narrowed his eyes and looked at his father. "And I don't think it was very nice, either!"

Suddenly he jumped up, turned round and stomped up the stairs to his room.

"Henry," said Mrs Buckett quietly, "I think you've got

some apologising to do, don't you?"

Mr Buckett sighed and hung his head. She was right, and he knew it. BJ didn't really mean to cause trouble. Suddenly he had an idea.

"I know," he thought. "Why don't I go and apologise to BJ – and ask him to help me think of a nice summer holiday that doesn't involve camping."

He shuddered. "I hate camping!"

Five minutes later, there was a knock at Johnny's bedroom door.

"Johnny? BJ? Can I come in?" asked Dad hopefully.

There was no reply.

Slowly, Dad opened the door and walked into the room. Johnny was lying on his bed listening to the radio, but BJ was nowhere to be seen.

"Where's BJ?"

"Johnny nodded towards the wardrobe. "In there."

Dad nodded. "Oh, thanks."

He walked quietly over to the wardrobe and pulled open the door. Inside, BJ was curled up on a pile of shirts, looking miserable.

"BJ," said Dad, clearly. "I've had a think about what I said. I've realised that I was wrong, and I apologise."

BJ looked up. "You don't mean that."

"Yes I do. And I want you to come on holiday with us."

"No you don't," said BJ, hoping that he did really.

Dad bent down and patted him on the head. "Yes I do, really."

BJ sat up, and blinked happily. "Really?" he asked.

"Yes!" replied Dad, for the third time.

"Yippee," cried BJ, jumping up and licking Dad's face.

"Did you hear that, Johnny? I'm going on holiday with you." He began to wag his tail violently from side to side, sending shirts shooting all over the room.

Dad burst out laughing. "And there's something else, BJ. I shall need your help. We've got to persuade Mum that we don't really want to go camping. I hate it. I want to go to a posh hotel and spend all the money we've got saved up and really enjoy myself."

"A hotel?" cried Johnny. "But dogs aren't allowed in hotels."

Dad nodded. "Yes, they are. Don't you worry, we'll find a nice hotel where they will let us take BJ."

He frowned. "Talking of which, what's that you're sitting on, BJ?"

"What's what?"

Dad leant down and picked up a brown envelope that had been hidden beneath the pile of shirts - until BJ scattered them with his tail. "It looks like a bill!" he said jokingly.

Then, he looked at the name on the front of the envelope - and gulped.

"It is a bill!" he gasped. "The telephone bill."

He bent down and pulled out another envelope, and then another, and then another. At the sight of each one, he groaned again.

"I don't believe it. There's a gas bill as well. And an electric bill... and a tax bill... and a credit card bill."

He scratched his head. "But I don't understand it -

how did all these bills get into your wardrobe, Johnny?"

Johnny shrugged. "I don't know."

BJ sat up proudly. "I put them there."

"But why?" asked Dad.

"Because," replied BJ, "you always get upset when you get bills. I thought you would be happier if you didn't get any. So every time I picked up the letters from the hallway, I hid your bills up here."

Dad groaned. "I don't believe it."

"Don't believe what?" asked Mum, who had just walked into the room.

Dad explained about the hidden bills.

Mum burst out laughing.

"It isn't funny," said Dad. "By the time I've paid all these bills, we won't be able to afford a summer holiday."

"Yes we will," replied Mum. "We'll just have to borrow Auntie Mary's tent and go camping like I said."

"Camping!" cried Johnny, excitedly. "Great."

"Yippee!" shouted BJ.

"Oh no," moaned Dad. "I hate camping."

Just then Johnny jumped off his bed and raced over to the radio. "Listen," he cried, turning it up to full volume. "They're playing our song."

Dad covered his ears. "It sounds awful. What is it?"

Johnny grinned. "It's a song by Cliff Richard. It's called 'We're all going on a Summer Holiday'."

Chapter 2

Time To Go!

Several weeks later, on the evening before they were due to set off on their camping holiday, there was a knock on Johnny's bedroom door.

"Come in," shouted Johnny and BJ together.

The door opened and Dad walked into the room, with his hands in his pockets. He smiled at Johnny, who was sitting reading in bed, and patted BJ on the head.

"Are you looking forward to tomorrow, then?" he asked.

Johnny put down the book he was reading, *The Camper's Handbook*, and nodded. "You bet!" he replied.

"What about you, BJ?" asked Dad.

BJ put down the piece of black cloth he was holding, and wagged his tail happily. "Can't wait." He sighed.

Dad smiled thoughtfully. "Good. I'm glad to hear it."

They were all silent for a few seconds.

"What about you, Dad?" asked Johnny, at last. "Are you looking forward to this holiday?"

His father nodded in silence.

"Really?" asked BJ, as if he didn't believe him.

Dad snorted. "Yes, of course I am. Why shouldn't I be?"

Johnny and BJ exchanged glances. Eventually, BJ coughed. "Because you said that you didn't like camping."

Dad pursed his lips and nodded again. "You're right. I did say that."

Johnny looked puzzled. "So why are you looking forward to going on holiday then, Dad? We're going camping."

"I know we are," replied his father. "But the way I look at it is this. I wanted to go somewhere hot and sunny – didn't I?"

Johnny and BJ both nodded.

"But we can't afford it – can we?"

Johnny and BJ both shook their heads.

"Which means," continued Dad, "that either we've got to go camping in Devon, or we've got to stay here at home for the rest of the holidays. Right?"

Johnny and BJ exchanged glances. This was starting to get a bit complicated. They weren't sure whether to agree or disagree.

"And according to the weather report," continued Dad, ignoring the confused looks on their faces, "for the next few days it's going to be cold and wet and miserable around here."

Johnny shuddered. He understood weather reports. He had done a project on them at school.

"Cold and wet and miserable," he echoed. "Sounds horrible!"

"Does it?" said BJ, who rather liked getting cold and wet.

"Of course it does!" said Dad, firmly "Which is why I'm looking forward to going camping in Devon. Because, according to the weather report, it's going to be lovely and hot and sunny down there, all week! See what I mean?"

He smiled at Johnny.

"I think I see what you mean," said Johnny slowly. He took a deep breath. "What you are saying is that you would rather spend a week camping in Devon, in the sunshine, than spend a week sitting in a cold, damp house feeling miserable."

Dad clapped him on the back happily. "That is precisely what I'm saying!"

"Oh," said Johnny. "Now I understand."

"Good," said his father. "Do you understand what I'm talking about, BJ?"

BJ shook his head. "No. But there again, I wasn't really listening – I've just lost my needle."

Dad frowned. "Your needle? What on earth were you doing with a needle?"

But before BJ could explain, Mum walked into the room carrying a bundle of clean washing. She put it down on the bed, next to Dad, and put her hands on her hips.

"Now listen to me, everybody," she said. "Don't forget, we're all doing our own packing for this holiday, so make sure that you take everything you need."

"I will," said Johnny, holding up his book. "There's a list in here that tells you everything that you could possibly need for a week's camping. So I'll use it to help me pack."

Dad snorted. "You don't need a list! Just use your common sense. That's all you need, isn't it, BJ?"

"Actually, I've got a list of things to pack as well," said BJ.

Dad snorted again. "I'm not surprised," he muttered. "You haven't got any common sense. You're a dog."

Mum held up her hands. "Oh, do be quiet, Henry. Stop trying to cause trouble."

Her husband tried to look innocent. "Me? Cause trouble?"

"Yes, and it's not going to work. We haven't got the time for it. As it happens," she continued, "I think it's a very good idea to have a list. I know I've drawn one up."

Her husband sighed. "Honestly, you lot are ridiculous." He shook his head. "You won't catch me wasting my time drawing up lists." He stood up and looked at his watch. "Now, if you will excuse me, I'm going to go and do my packing – and I can guarantee you two things."

He looked at Mum purposefully. "One, I won't forget anything. And two, I won't need a list!"

He walked out of the room, still shaking his head and muttering to himself that he was obviously the only one in the household with any common sense.

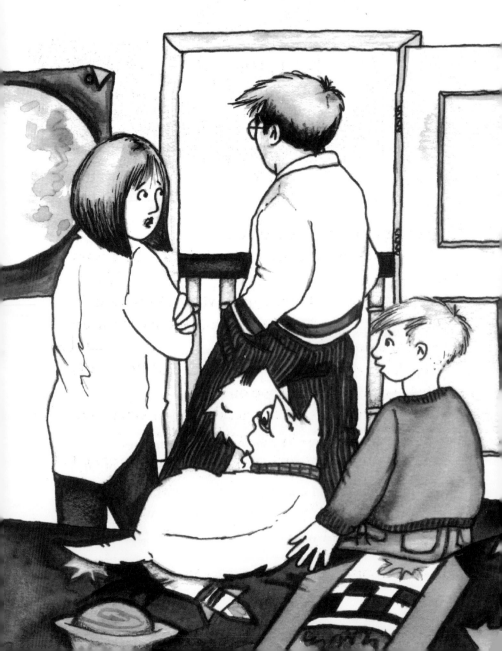

When he had gone, Mum sighed.

"He's bound to leave something behind – he always does!"

She bent down. "Talking of leaving things behind, someone's left a needle on the floor." She picked it up and placed it on Johnny's desk.

"Thank goodness you've found it," said BJ. "I was worried in case someone stood on it."

"Well, luckily they didn't," said Mum. "But what were you doing with a needle in the first place, BJ?"

BJ coughed. "I was making something," he replied proudly.

"What?" asked Mum.

"A monocle case."

"What on earth for?"

BJ looked surprised. "My monocle – what else?"

Before Mum could reply, he remembered something that he wanted to ask her. "I say," he said, "do you have a piece of card that I could use?"

Mum frowned at him. "Pardon?"

"I said, do you have a piece of card that I could use?"

"What for?" asked Mum.

BJ held up the piece of black cloth he was working on.

"My monocle case. I need a piece of card to stiffen the back."

"Really?"

"Yes."

"How big does this piece of card have to be?" asked Mum.

BJ thought for a moment. "A bit bigger than a matchbox," he said.

"All right," said Mum. "I'll see what I can find for you later. Right now I think we should all take a leaf out of Dad's book, and get on with our packing."

And with that she left the room.

The next morning after breakfast, Dad went and got the car out of the garage. Then he put on the roof rack and opened the boot.

"Right," he said. "First things first. We need to get the roof rack packed. The question is, what with?" He scratched his chin, and surveyed the pile of bags, boxes and suitcases lying in the hallway.

After a moment's careful thought, he picked up the two largest suitcases and took them outside to the car, where he lifted them onto the roof rack. Then he came back and picked up the green canvas sack which held the tent.

"Johnny," he said. "Could you give me a hand, please?"

Johnny, who was sitting on the stairs watching, stood up and nodded. "Sure thing, Dad. What can I do for you?"

"Carry the rest of these things out to the car while I get this on the roof rack."

"OK, Dad."

So, whilst Dad busied himself strapping the tent and suitcases securely into position, Johnny began carrying an assortment of bags and boxes and bits out to the driveway, where he placed them on the concrete next to the car.

"Johnny," said his father. "Have you seen BJ recently?"

"Yes." Johnny put down the bag he was holding and stretched out his arms. "He's in your bedroom finishing off his monocle case."

"His what?"

"His monocle case – he's scared that his monocle will get scratched in the tent, so he's making a case to protect it."

Dad snorted. "That dog! He does the strangest things sometimes. What will he think of next?" He climbed down from the side of the car and surveyed the neat pile strapped to the roof rack.

"Still," he said thoughtfully. "As long as it keeps him out of trouble, and out of my way, I'm not going to complain! Come on, let's see if there's anything else to be packed."

Together, he and Johnny went into the house.

Fifteen minutes later, they were all packed and ready to go. The pile of bags, boxes and bits had been squeezed into the boot of the car, and all four members of the Buckett household had been squeezed into their seat belts.

"Right, is everybody ready?" asked Dad, putting the key into the ignition.

"Yes," shouted Johnny. "Let's go."

"Rather," added BJ.

"No," replied Mum. "Let's not go just yet – I'm not ready."

Dad looked puzzled. "What do you mean, you're not ready? You must be, we're all packed."

"That's exactly what I mean. How do you know we're all packed?" asked Mum.

"Because I packed the car," replied Dad. "And I didn't leave anything out."

Mum sighed. "Look," she said, "every year you pack the car – and every year, you leave something behind, don't you?"

Dad opened his mouth, and was just about to disagree when Mum held up her hand for silence.

"For instance," she said firmly, "last year you forgot the passports."

Dad quickly closed his mouth.

She was right.

"And the year before that," continued Mum, "you forgot to bring the tickets – and we had to wait over four hours before they would let us on the ferry."

Dad gulped.

She was right again.

"And the year before that," said Mum, "Was the worst ever. You actually managed to forget the..."

"All right," said Dad, quickly "I get your point. I admit that I do have a habit of forgetting one or two little things when I pack the car to go on holiday."

Mum looked at him and raised her eyebrows.

"OK, OK!" Dad held up his arms as though to surrender. "I do have a habit of forgetting one or two very important things whenever I pack the car to go on holiday."

"And the trouble is," muttered Mum, "that we never

realise you've forgotten them until it's too late to go back and get them!"

Dad hung his head, and looked sheepish.

"So I think that this year, we should double check that you actually have packed everything we need."

Dad gulped nervously. "What do you mean – double check? You mean, unpack everything and then pack it all back in again?"

Mum sighed. "Of course not. What I mean is, that we should go through my list, item by item, making sure that somebody..." she stared at her husband. "...hasn't left anything behind."

At this point BJ, who had been staring at his newly completed monocle case and listening in silence, jumped up. "I think that's a very good idea!" he said, wagging his tail.

Dad groaned. "You would."

"Come on, Dad," said Johnny. "You have to admit, Mum's got a point."

"You too, Johnny?" groaned Dad.

He took the keys out of the ignition and sat back in his seat. "All right," he said. "Let's go through this list. But I warn you – I haven't forgotten anything this year, honest!"

"We'll soon see about that," said Mum, pulling out her list and pen. "Item one – the tent."

"Packed," said Dad.

"Item two – sleeping bags."

"Packed," said Dad.

"Item three – pillows."

"Packed."

"Item four ..."

Two hours and a hundred and sixty kilometres later, Dad slowed the car down and pulled into a service station.

"I need to stretch my legs," he said. "We need some petrol too."

He drove the car into the garage and stopped next to a convenient petrol pump. Then he climbed out and took the top off the fuel tank of the car.

When the tank was full to overflowing Dad switched off the pump and walked into the petrol station to pay the lady behind the desk.

Two minutes later he was back again, looking embarrassed.

"I don't believe it," he hissed. "I have forgotten something."

"What?" asked Mum, starting to look worried.

"My money," replied Dad.

Mum relaxed. "No, you haven't. We decided not to bring any money with us this time, remember? We're going to pay for everything with the credit card. Don't worry – I've got it in my purse."

"Thank goodness for that," sighed Dad. "I was worried there for a minute."

"I'm not surprised," chuckled Mum, picking up her handbag. She put her hand inside it, took out her purse and opened it carefully.

Then she looked inside.

The colour left her face.

"Aaargh!" she screamed.

"What is it?" asked Dad. "What's wrong?"

"I - I -," Mum gulped. "I haven't got it!"

"What?" cried Dad. "You haven't got the credit card? Why not? Where is it?"

"I don't know!"

Suddenly, Mum gasped. "Oh, no!"

She closed her eyes and gritted her teeth.

"I know what you're going to say, Henry. And you're right. It's all my fault. The truth is - I forgot to pack it. It's lying on my chest of drawers."

"You forgot to pack the credit card?" squeaked Dad. "After giving me that huge great lecture about not forgetting things, you forgot to pack the credit card?"

He shook his head in amazement. "But that means we can't pay for the petrol!"

He collapsed against the side of the car.

"And we haven't got any money! I don't believe it."

Mum shook her head. "Nor do I."

"I say," said BJ. "Did you say that this credit card of yours was lying on your chest of drawers?"

Mum nodded. "Yes, it is."

"You mean, it was," said BJ. "You remember I asked you if I could have a piece of card?"

Mum nodded. "Oh yes, so you did, BJ. I'm sorry, I forgot to look it out for you. But I'm too busy to think about that just now."

BJ pulled something out from underneath him.

"No you're not," he said. "Because I didn't realise that you had forgotten. When I saw that credit card lying on your chest of drawers, I thought it was for my monocle case."

There was silence for a few long seconds.

"So?" said Mum hopefully.

"So," BJ grinned, "your credit card is right here in my monocle case."

"Brilliant," cried Johnny. "Well done, BJ."

"You know what this means, don't you, BJ?" said Mum, kissing him on the head.

"No," said BJ. "What does it mean?"

"It means that you're a hero," said Dad. "You've saved us all. Without that credit card, we would have been in real trouble!"

Mum nodded. "It also means something else, Henry."

"What?" asked her husband.

"That I owe you an apology. You were right about drawing up lists. It's a waste of time!"

Chapter 3

At The Seaside

The next morning, after the Buckett family had woken up, got dressed and had breakfast, they all climbed out of the tent. They were immediately bathed in the hot sunshine outside.

"This," said Dad, sitting down in his deckchair, "is definitely the life for me. I've changed my mind about camping – it's actually very enjoyable." He nodded to himself happily.

"Very enjoyable," he repeated.

He stretched out his arms and closed his eyes.

"Hmm," he sighed. "Very, very, enjoyable."

"I quite agree," said BJ. He lay down on the warm grass, and yawned. "My only complaint is about the noise."

"So you heard it too, did you?" asked Johnny, who was lying on his back staring up at the clear blue sky overhead.

"Rather," replied BJ. "It kept me awake for half the night."

Johnny rolled over and leant on his elbow. "Hey, it kept me awake for half the night as well. It sounded like a chainsaw that was about to explode, didn't it?"

BJ nodded.

"It made the tent shake," continued Johnny. "I actually thought it was going to fall down for a while."

BJ frowned. "I wonder what it was, and where it was coming from."

Johnny shrugged and put a blade of grass in his mouth. "I don't know," he said. "It didn't sound human though, did it?"

"No!" BJ shook his head so violently that his monocle dropped off.

"I expect it was some animal in the field next door," continued Johnny. "A cow, or a horse, or something like that."

Mum put down the book she was reading and cleared her throat quietly.

"You know what, Johnny, you're exactly half-right."

"Huh?" Johnny looked puzzled. "What do you mean – half-right, Mum?"

"I mean – it was an animal making that noise in the night. But it wasn't in the field next door. It was inside the tent."

"You mean there was an animal in the tent with us, all night?" gasped Johnny. "What sort of animal?"

His mother tilted her head towards her sleeping husband.

"That sort of animal!"

Johnny sat up, looking shocked. "You mean that dreadful, horrible noise - was Dad?"

Mum nodded. "He always makes that noise - when he snores."

"That was Dad - snoring? I can't believe it!" muttered Johnny in disbelief.

At that moment, a loud noise split the air.

It sounded like a chainsaw about to explode.

And it was coming out of Dad's mouth.

Johnny covered his ears, and pulled a face. "Actually, I take that back," he groaned. "I can believe it."

BJ, who had picked up his monocle and put it back in its place, stared at Dad.

He looked amazed.

"I say," he said, eventually, "that really is incredible. I would never have thought it possible for one man to make so much noise - whilst he's asleep!"

He licked his lips. "I've got to take a closer look!"

He jumped up onto Dad's lap, and squinted up at the open mouth above him. He stared, fascinated, at Dad's wobbling tonsils. He leant further and further forward, until at last, his monocle was touching Dad's slobbery wet lips.

At that point, two things happened.

One, Dad screamed and jumped up out of his chair, and two, BJ promptly fell onto the floor with a grunt!

"Help!" cried Dad. "Something's just flown into my mouth!"

He put his hand up to his mouth and pulled out a round, flat object – BJ's monocle.

He stared at it, and then scowled at BJ – who was rolling around on the grass, clutching his tummy and roaring with laughter.

"What's so funny?" demanded Dad.

"Hehehe," giggled BJ. "Your tonsils wobble when you snore!"

"Pardon?" Dad looked suitably confused.

"You were snoring," explained Johnny helpfully.

"Oh no I wasn't."

"Oh yes you were!" chimed Johnny and BJ together.

"When?" asked Dad.

"Just now," said BJ cheerfully.

"Nonsense," replied Dad. "I was wide awake."

Johnny grinned. "Dad," he said. "How on earth can you have been wide awake?" He burst out laughing. "You had your eyes closed, and you were snoring!"

Dad raised his eyebrows. "As it happens," he said slowly, "I was thinking..."

Mum snorted. "Thinking, my foot. You were asleep, Henry. You're always falling asleep these days."

"No, I'm not," Dad rubbed his eyes. "And anyway, I never snore."

"You always snore," continued his wife, ignoring him and going back to her book.

"I am not always falling sleep – and I did not snore!" Dad stamped his foot. "So there!"

"You know what?" said Mum, without looking up. "You really sound like a toddler sometimes, Henry Buckett."

Dad stamped his foot again. "Oh no I don't."

Mum sighed. "See what I mean? Anyway, I'm not going to argue about it – I want to know what we're going to do today."

"Let's go to the seaside," cried Dad, jumping to his feet. "I want to build a sandcastle."

Mum looked at Johnny and BJ, and sighed. "He is just like a great big toddler. Isn't he?"

Johnny and BJ nodded silently.

Before Dad could say a word, Mum stood up. "But I think he's right, anyway. We should go to the beach and enjoy the sunshine. According to this little guide book I've been reading, there's a lovely sandy beach just along the coast."

"Yippee!" cried Johnny.

"Let's go," added BJ.

"I don't snore," muttered Dad. "And I'm not always falling asleep."

Half an hour later, the entire Buckett family were clambering down a flight of steps which led on to the lovely sandy beach that Mum had read about.

"Where shall we go, then?" asked Mum.

"What about over there," cried Johnny, pointing, "by all those people building sandcastles?"

"All right, let's go."

After they had arrived at the spot Johnny had pointed out, they put down all the bags and buckets and spades they were carrying, and went off to explore.

Johnny and BJ went one way, whilst Dad went the other. Mum stayed behind to lie in the sun and get brown.

Five minutes later, Johnny and BJ were back again.

"Mum, can we have an ice-cream?" asked Johnny.

Mum, who had got changed into her swimsuit and was lying flat out on an enormous beach towel, sighed.

"No, Johnny, you can't. I didn't bring any money, I'm afraid."

Johnny looked thoughtful. "Can we enter the Sandcastle Competition, then?" he asked. "It's free, and the first prize is ten pounds."

Mum leant up on one elbow. "In that case, yes, you can enter the competition. What have you got to do – build a sandcastle, I suppose?"

BJ wagged his tail and nodded. "Yes, and I've never built a sandcastle before. I'm really excited."

"It doesn't have to be a sandcastle, BJ," said Johnny. "The man said you could build anything you like." He frowned. "What was the phrase he used?"

"Sand Sculpture," said BJ. "He said that if you didn't

want to do a sandcastle, you could always do a Sand Sculpture."

"That's right," agreed Johnny. "Well, that's what I think we should do. It sounds more exciting."

"OK," agreed BJ.

Mum lay down again, and sighed. "I'll be right here if you need me," she said. "Don't go too far away, will you?"

"Of course not," said Johnny. "We don't need to. We're going to build it just over there." He pointed to a spot a few metres away from where Mum was lying.

"Good luck," said Mum, closing her eyes... and wishing that everyone would go away and leave her alone.

All she really wanted to do was sunbathe.

Johnny and BJ disappeared.

Shortly afterwards, Dad reappeared.

"Guess what I've found!" he said, full of excitement.

"What?" said Mum, trying to sound interested, even though she wasn't.

"A paddling pool," replied Dad. He looked thoughtful. "I wonder if Johnny and BJ want to come and play in it?"

"I doubt it – they're entering the Sandcastle Competition. They're building a Sand Sculpture."

Dad shrugged. "Fair enough, it's their loss. I'll go by myself."

He bent down and rolled up his trousers, then turned to go. Suddenly he had an idea.

"And when I come back, I'll go and get some ice-creams."

Mum was just about to remind him that they didn't have any money with them, when he walked off, whistling happily to himself.

She decided not to bother.

"At last," she sighed. "Peace, blessed peace."

Ten minutes later, Mum heard the sound of squelching footsteps coming towards her. She opened her eyes and saw a strange-looking man standing next to her towel.

It was Dad.

He had stopped whistling, and he looked far from happy.

In fact, he looked wet.

Very wet.

Mum sat up. "What have you been doing, Henry?"

"Getting wet."

"I can see that." Mum frowned. "The question is – why?"

"Because I fell over."

"Fell over?" echoed Mum. "In a paddling pool? How?"

Dad shivered. "I was having a hopping race with myself – and I slipped."

Mum shook her head. "You really are a toddler, aren't you, Henry?"

Her husband sniffed.

"Anyway," said Mum briskly. "The first thing you should do is get out of those sopping clothes and dry yourself."

Dad nodded. "You're right."

Slowly, he peeled off his soaking wet trousers and T-shirt, to reveal dripping wet swimming trunks beneath. Then, he picked up a beach towel and began to rub himself dry, violently.

Drops of water shot everywhere.

"Henry," said his wife. "Be careful! You're soaking me!"

"Sorry, dear." Dad took a couple of steps away from his wife, and moved closer towards the spot where Johnny and BJ were busily sculpting a mermaid out of sand.

"I'm going to have a lie down," said Dad. "I need a rest after all that excitement."

His wife smiled. "All right, Henry. Just make sure that you don't snore too loudly."

Dad looked hurt. "I won't fall asleep – and I never snore!"

"Of course, I forgot," Mum looked thoughtful. "You don't fall asleep all the time, do you?"

Dad lay down on his towel, put his sunhat over his face, and closed his eyes. "No."

"So why are you closing your eyes, then?" asked Mum, innocently picking up a nearby bucket and spade.

"Because I'm thinking," replied Dad.

Two minutes later he was fast asleep, and Mum got busy with her bucket and spade.

She had decided to make a Sand Sculpture of her own...

Twenty minutes later, Johnny and BJ came over to where Mum was putting the finishing touches to her sculpture.

"Wow," breathed Johnny. "That's brilliant, Mum."

"It certainly is," agreed BJ. "I can't think why, but it reminds me of something."

"Some one, more like," muttered Mum.

"Hey," said Johnny, looking all around. "Where's Dad? I haven't seen him for ages. I wonder what he's doing?"

"I know what he's doing," laughed Mum. She stood up and looked down at her Sand Sculpture. "He's thinking!"

Just then, an old man wearing a gold chain appeared.

"And who made this fascinating sculpture?" he asked.

"I did," replied Mum. "Why do you ask?"

"Because I'm judging the Sandcastle Competition – and I've decided that this one is the winner." He handed Mum a ten pound note. "And here's your prize."

Johnny gasped. "Well done, Mum."

"Does it have a title?" asked the old man.

"Pardon?" asked Mum, who was trying hard not to laugh.

"What is your Sand Sculpture called?"

Mum thought for a minute. She was just about to speak, when a strange noise split the air.

It sounded like a chainsaw about to explode.

And it came from underneath the sunhat which covered the Sand Sculpture's face.

"Dad!" cried Johnny.

The old man nodded. "That's a very good name for it." He wrote something down on a piece of paper, and strolled off towards the rest of the Sandcastle Competition.

"I don't believe it," giggled BJ. "You turned Dad into a Sand Sculpture."

Mum nodded. "Yes, I did. And before we scrape all the sand off him and change him back into an ordinary Dad – there are two things we've got to do."

"What?" asked Johnny.

"First," said Mum picking up her camera, "we've got to take a picture of your father. I'll be needing it later."

"What for?" asked BJ.

"To shut him up next time he tries to tell us that he doesn't fall asleep all the time!"

There was silence as Mum took a photograph.

"And what's the second thing we've got to do?" asked Johnny, after a few seconds.

Mum grinned. "We've got to go and spend this ten pounds," she said, waving her prize. "Who wants an ice-cream?"

"Me!" yelled Johnny and BJ together.

Arm in arm in paw, they set off for the ice-cream shop.

Chapter 4

The Barbecue That Wasn't

The next morning, when Mr Buckett stuck his head out of the tent, the clear blue sky of yesterday had been replaced by banks of fluffy white clouds.

"What's the weather like, dear?" asked his wife from inside her sleeping bag.

"Not so good!" replied Dad, coming back into the tent looking glum.

Mum smiled. "That's a pity – I was hoping to go back to the beach today." She licked her lips, the way she always did when she was about to tease her husband. "I was thinking of making another Sand Sculpture..."

She looked at her husband hopefully.

She didn't really want to go to the beach at all, or make a Sand Sculpture; she just wanted to see her husband's reaction to the idea.

She didn't have to wait long.

As soon as she had finished speaking, Dad shuddered. Suddenly he was glad that the weather had changed for

the worse. He had had enough of sun, sea and Sand Sculptures to last him a lifetime.

"Yes, it is a pity we can't go to the beach, isn't it?" he said, sounding very relieved that they couldn't.

He picked up his socks and began to examine them carefully.

"So," asked Johnny through a mouthful of cornflakes. "What are we going to do today, then?"

"I say, we could always go out for a walk," said a muffled voice from the other side of the tent. "Then, when we come back, we could have a barbecue."

Johnny frowned. "BJ? What are you doing?"

BJ's tail came into sight, followed closely by BJ, who was chewing something that looked suspiciously like a tent peg.

"I'm having a bite to eat – I've just found a whole load of these really tasty sticks." BJ grinned. "That's what gave me the idea for a barbecue. They're delicious."

Johnny was just about to ask whether the sticks really were, in fact, tent pegs, when Dad jumped into the air with a shout.

"I've just had a brilliant idea," he cried, throwing down his socks. "Why don't we go for a walk?"

Johnny and BJ exchanged glances.

"Then," continued Dad happily, "When we come back, we could have a barbecue."

Mum nodded. "That is an excellent idea, Henry."

Her husband smiled.

"Which is probably why BJ thought of it about two minutes before you did," continued Mum. She raised her eyebrows and looked at her husband quizzically. "Isn't it?"

Mr Buckett looked surprised. "Did you really, BJ?"

BJ nodded. He couldn't reply because his mouth was full of tent peg.

Mr Buckett laughed. "It just shows you, doesn't it, dear? Great minds really do think alike. Don't we, BJ?"

Mum did not look convinced. "Well, both of your great minds seem to have forgotten one tiny detail."

"What's that?" asked Dad, with a smile.

"The weather forecast we heard on the radio last night," said Mum, quietly. "It said that today it was going to be cloudy at first, with rainy showers later and a force six wind. In other words, not exactly the weather for walks or barbecues."

"Maybe we should do something else, then," ventured BJ.

"Rubbish!" snorted Dad. "What do weathermen know? Nothing, that's what." He stuck his head back out of the tent and looked up at the sky.

"Trust me – it won't rain today." He took a deep breath of cool, moist air. "In fact," he continued, "I think it's going to end up being even sunnier, lovelier and hotter than yesterday!"

Mum still did not look convinced. "I think we should go for a swim," she said firmly. "According to my guide book, there's a lovely new leisure centre just down the road from our campsite – with a swimming pool, wave machine and everything."

Dad looked unimpressed.

"And," continued Mum, "it's all under cover. So our day won't be spoiled by the rain."

Dad looked even more unimpressed.

Mum sighed. "Honestly, Henry, you're acting like a toddler again!"

"I don't want to go swimming," grumbled Dad. "I've had enough of getting wet for this holiday."

"What do you mean, Dad?" asked Johnny, who had now finished his breakfast and was getting dressed.

"Nothing," said Dad quickly. He hadn't told Johnny and BJ about the paddling pool incident – and he didn't want to.

It was too embarrassing.

"Your father fell over in a paddling pool yesterday," whispered Mum. "While you and BJ were sculpting your mermaid."

"He fell over? How?" asked Johnny in amazement.

"He was having a hopping race," replied Mum.

"Who with?" asked BJ, who had finished chewing his tent peg and was busy polishing his monocle.

"Himself!"

Johnny grinned. "You weren't, were you, Dad?"

His father coughed, and tried to look innocent. As if he would never have a hopping race against himself - especially not in a paddling pool.

It didn't work.

BJ giggled, and Dad went bright red from the neck up.

"I," said Dad, crawling hurriedly towards the door of the tent, "am going out for a walk. I don't know if anyone would like to join me. And to be honest, I don't really care."

After he had gone, Mum, Johnny and BJ all looked at one another in silence.

"I think your father is a bit embarrassed," said Mum, eventually.

Johnny nodded. "I think you're right," he agreed.

"And I think," said BJ, firmly, "that we should all go out for a walk. It will make Dad feel better if he is in charge - for once."

"I have to agree," sighed Mum. "But I also think that we should all take our cagoules, just in case it does decide to rain. The weather reports aren't always wrong, you know."

Shortly afterwards, the entire Buckett family, with Dad at the head, set off for a walk along the cliffs.

Two hours later, they stopped outside a shop that seemed to sell everything. There were postcards, buckets and spades, baked beans, ice-creams and sandwiches.

"Stop," cried Dad, holding up a hand. He was enjoying being the boss for once – it made him feel important. He pointed to the shop. "I think it's about time for lunch."

"Yes please," cried Johnny, staring at the ice-creams.

"Rather," added BJ, wagging his tail and thinking of baked beans.

"I agree," said Mum. "We could all do with a nice, sensible sandwich. Couldn't we?"

"A sandwich?" echoed Johnny sadly. "Why can't we have an ice-cream?"

"Or a tin of cold baked beans?" added BJ.

"Because neither of them are Good For You," said Mum firmly.

She had a thing about food. She didn't approve of it unless it was Good For You.

Johnny sighed. As far as he could work out, his mother only thought that food was Good For You if you didn't enjoy eating it.

"Baked beans are Good For You," said BJ hopefully.

"Not when they're cold," said Mum, very firmly. She opened the door of the shop for Dad. "Come on, boss. Let's go and get ourselves some sandwiches." She walked into the shop and out of sight.

Surprisingly, when she was gone, Dad nodded his approval. "Mum's right, you know," he said. "We need

something sensible to fill us up and give us energy for the afternoon ahead."

Johnny looked suitably surprised. "Dad," he said, "since when have you started liking sensible food?"

"Since I became the boss!" said Dad. He smiled and followed his wife into the shop.

Johnny and BJ exchanged glances.

"You know what I think?" said Johnny.

"What?" asked BJ.

"I think Dad is actually growing up!"

BJ shrugged. "It had to happen one day, didn't it?"

Five minutes later, Mum and Dad came back out of the shop, each holding a large plastic bag.

"There you are," said Mum handing out sandwiches, apples and raisins. "We can sit over there on that bench and have a picnic lunch."

"Good idea," said Dad.

They all went over to the bench, sat down, and began to eat their lunch.

"I'm still hungry," said Johnny when he had finished his last mouthful. He looked up at the darkening sky overhead and shivered. "And I'm cold."

Dad stood up. "In that case, I suggest that we carry on with our walk. That'll soon warm you up."

"But it won't stop me being hungry, will it?"

"You're right there," agreed Dad. "It won't. But I know what will stop you being hungry."

"What?" asked Johnny, gritting his teeth against the chill wind that had sprung up.

"Hot dogs!" replied his father.

"Hot dogs!" repeated Johnny, immediately sounding more cheerful. "Yes, please. I could eat a dozen."

BJ looked up from his dinner. "Pardon?" He looked worried.

Mum laughed. "It's all right, BJ. We're not talking about eating dogs."

BJ looked relieved. "So, what are you talking about, then?" he asked.

"Sausage sandwiches," replied Mum. "We call them hot dogs." She stood up. "Shall we go?"

BJ groaned. "More sandwiches."

"Don't worry, BJ," hissed Johnny. "You'll love hot dogs. They're delicious." He rubbed his hands together. "So, where do we get them from, Dad?"

"In here." Dad pointed to the plastic bag at his feet.

"What?" squawked Johnny. "They'll be getting cold."

"No, they won't. See?" Dad reached into the bag and drew out a packet of sausages and a packet of white rolls. "We're going to barbecue them when we get back to the tent."

Johnny wrapped himself up tighter in his jacket and frowned.

"A barbecue? In this weather? There's a freezing wind and it looks as if it's going to rain."

BJ nodded. "It looks as if the weather report was right, after all."

Dad smiled. "Oh, you of little faith," he said. "You just wait, by the time we get back to the tent, the weather will have changed. It'll be perfect for barbecues." He held up his finger and smiled.

"Remember, the boss always knows best!"

Two minutes later they set off on the two hour trek back to the tent.

By the time they arrived back at the campsite, Dad had been proved at least half-right - the weather had changed. The trouble was, that it had changed for the worse.

"I think we had better give the barbecue a miss, dear," said Mum as a drop of rain fell onto her hand.

"Nonsense," replied Dad. "It's only a shower. It'll soon stop. You three go into the tent and I'll get the barbecue started." He smiled confidently. "I'll call you when it's ready."

Mum was just about to argue, when BJ winked at her through his monocle. She frowned and wondered why.

She didn't have to wait long to find out.

"Follow me," whispered BJ. They went into the tent, followed by Johnny.

"The truth is," whispered BJ, "the weather report was right. It said it would be cold, wet and windy... and it is – isn't it?"

Mum and Johnny nodded.

"So Dad was wrong, wasn't he?"

Mum and Johnny nodded again.

"But," continued BJ. "I don't think we should say anything. Even though we all got frozen on the walk, and it's far too cold to stand around outside having a barbecue, we shouldn't say a thing."

"Why not?" asked Johnny. "He's mad. Mum was right, we should have gone swimming."

"I know," agreed BJ. "The thing is, he's been so happy being the boss all day. We shouldn't spoil it for him."

Mum sighed. "I think you're both right. Dad is enjoying being boss and we should have gone swimming."

"But we couldn't, could we?" said Johnny. "Because Dad didn't want to get wet."

"Exactly," said Mum. "Which is why I think we should do as BJ says, and go along with your father's strange ideas. He hasn't had a very good holiday so far, what with snoring, falling over in the paddling pool, and being made into a sand sculpture. The least we could do is humour him, isn't it?"

"I suppose so," agreed Johnny, grudgingly.

"Of course it is," said BJ. "Anyway, I think it's time for us all to go out and enjoy the barbecue. Come on."

With that, they all climbed out of the tent, trying their best to look as if they were looking forward to eating hot dogs in a freezing force six wind.

"You see," cried Dad happily. "I told you that it wouldn't last."

"What?" asked Mum - watching the tent as it flapped in the breeze. For some reason it didn't seem to be attached to the ground as much as it should be.

"The rain," said Dad. "It's stopped. Here, take this." He handed Mum a hot dog.

Mum took a bite from her hot dog and looked up at the sky. Dad was right - the rain had stopped. But the wind hadn't. If anything it had got worse.

"I wish this wind would stop," muttered Mum. "It's blowing my hair all over the place." She watched as one edge of the tent lifted clean off the ground. "And it looks as if it wants to blow the tent all over the place as well."

"Do you want any mustard?" asked Dad.

"Yes please."

Dad crawled into the tent to get the mustard jar.

"Johnny," said Mum, quietly. "Does the tent look all right to you?"

Johnny looked at the tent, and then frowned. "No, it doesn't. It looks loose - as if someone's taken out all the tent pegs." He stopped. "Oh no."

"What?" asked Mum.

"BJ!" cried Johnny. "Those sticks you were chewing this morning - where did you get them from?"

BJ swallowed the mouthful of hot dog he was eating and blinked. He looked as if he couldn't believe what he was seeing. "Those sticks?" he said vaguely. "Oh, they were stuck in the ground all round the outside of the tent."

Johnny groaned. "BJ, those were the tent pegs!"

"So?" By now BJ was staring at the tent in disbelief.

"So without them, there's nothing holding the tent down. It could blow away at any minute."

"Really?"

"Yes," said Johnny. "Really."

"In that case," said BJ, sounding relieved, "perhaps my eyes aren't playing tricks on me, after all."

"What do you mean - playing tricks on you?" asked Mum.

"Well," said BJ. "When I saw that the tent was moving - I thought I was seeing things. But obviously I wasn't. The tent really is moving."

He watched as the tent sailed gracefully across the campsite towards a large fishing pond.

"What do you mean - moving?" asked Mum, turning to look at the tent. She squealed.

"Henry, watch out!" But it was too late.

With a gentle whoosh, the tent hit the pond - and sank.

Mum frowned. "You know what I think?" she said.

"No," said Johnny and BJ together. "What?"

"I think that the next time your father suggests we all go for a walk and then have a barbecue - we should go swimming instead."

They all watched as Dad climbed out of the pond and shook himself, sending water flying everywhere.

"You know what I think?" said BJ.

"No," said Mum and Johnny together. "What?"

"I think that Dad would agree with you!"